IN THE COMPANY OF WRITERS 2009

MEADOW BROOK WRITING PROJECT 2009 SUMMER INSTITUTE

iUniverse, Inc.
New York   Bloomington

In the Company of Writers 2009

iUniverse books may be ordered through booksellers or by contacting:

iUniverse
1663 Liberty Drive
Bloomington, IN 47403
www.iuniverse.com
1-800-Authors (1-800-288-4677)

ISBN: 978-1-4502-5937-8 (pbk)
ISBN: 978-1-4502-5936-1 (ebk)

Credit for interior images: Dover Electronic Clip Art Series, Dover Publications, Inc
Printed in the United States of America

iUniverse rev. date: 10/19/10

CONTENTS

Acknowledgements

On behalf of the Summer Institute teacher-consultants and authors of this book, its editors, Art Orme and Shaun Moore, would like to thank the Meadow Brook Writing Project for affording us the opportunity to experience in July 2009 an intensive month of professional development, teachers teaching teachers and writers writing with writers. We owe a special thank you as well to the following persons for helping us to make this book possible: Professor Marshall Kitchens, acting director of the Meadow Brook Writing Project. Co-directors Mary Cox and Kathleen Reddy-Butkovich. Cliff Lawson for his technical assistance with the graphics. Kathleen Lawson for help with the graphics, editing, and her assistance in general.

PREFACE

The Commitment

Halleemah couldn't sleep a wink the night before the Meadow Brook Writing Project. With every toss and turn she wondered who the other participants were and if she were worthy to be in the company of those who deemed themselves writers. For as long as Halleemah could remember, she questioned her worth and capabilities. So the insecure feeling that haunted her on her drive the morning of July 6 was nothing new.

At 8:45 am, she reached her destination. It was the first day of the Writing Project, and though she was very excited, Halleemah feared what might lie ahead. Taking a deep long breath, she closed her eyes and walked through the door. There sat eight strangers in a room so silent, they probably could hear the pitter patters of her heart.

"Wonderful. Eight overachievers. It starts at nine. I'm here at 8:45, and I'm the late one!" Halleemah grumbled as she eyed each name tag one by one.

Hoping that one of them would tell her how to get one of the name doodads, she psyched herself out to search for one of her own. Blue sheets of paper and markers were at the head of the table, and with a swift look to her left and right, Halleemah grabbed them and ran right back to her seat. After crafting a delightful name signature, she tried every elementary fold she knew, but couldn't get it to stand up like the others. It wasn't even nine o' clock yet, and it was proven that she was way out of her league! She didn't even notice the pre-folded name tags in the center of the table.

Just as Halleemah contemplated going home to her new baby, a frantic late comer tickled her fancy. "I'm not the only one who thinks time is overrated," she sighed. As the morning activities began to unfold, the apprehensive teacher from Hamtramck made a private vow to stay. The butterflies that once filled her stomach were replaced with a sense of urgency to be in the company of writers.

by Holly L. Gilbert-Ryle

FOREWORD

"Writing in its many forms is the signature means of communication in the 21st century. The National Writing Project envisions a future where every person is an accomplished writer, engaged learner and active participant in a digital interconnected world."

The official mission statement of the National Writing Project is an ambitious undertaking, requiring dedication and a willingness to share and learn from colleagues. To that end, we, the twelve members of the Summer Institute of Oakland University's Meadow Brook Writing Project, spent the month of July 2009 sharing ideas and donuts, while learning new technologies and enjoying what we do best—writing and teaching.

What follows are the combined results of our explorations into the wonderful world of words.

by Art Orme

CHAPTER 1

Darlene Marshall

Not for Sale

After visiting The Chair for many months, she and I had developed quite an affinity for each other, so I decided it was time to introduce her to my daughter. Cassidy, too, fell in love, and we began visiting The Chair as most go to visit grandma or an old friend for tea.

But the tag always read the same: PROPERTY OF STORE. NOT FOR SALE. It was a Salvation Army Thrift Store. It had a big sign that read, "Donations in the Back." DONATIONS. To help those less fortunate. How could something not be for sale in a thrift store, a charitable one, no less? It just did not compute.

It was on this day I decided to pull out the soapbox which I conveniently carried in my back pocket, and ask for someone in charge. Lucky visit eleven. Lucky Mary Lou.

As she approached from the back of the store, she pulled a Kool from her front pocket, though she easily could have gone to her left shoulder, to either of the packs trapped under her shirt sleeve. "What item you interested in?" She rasped, sucking in her cheeks to further ignite the dangling stick.

"The pink chair." I looked her straight in the eye, bending her to my will. I had always wondered what happened to the narrator of *Tales from the Crypt*. The Cryptkeeper, it seemed, was alive and well, and not selling pink chairs from the resale shop.

The "item" Store Manager Mary Lou had referenced so casually was one of the great wonders of the world, a priceless artifact tucked into a corner of that singular treasure chest known as the Salvation Army Thrift Store. Each time I visited this incredibly rendered work of art, I fell more in love with her every detail. She was pink like deep bubble gum. She swirled like only 1970s art deco chairs can, like winding stairs to funky town. She was clothed in the kind of cheap velour you just can't find nowadays, and she still had the imprint of fat weave polyester from discoing butts of years gone by. She spoke to me, karmically. Andy

Warhol would have painted this chair to preserve her import forever. I took her in the way I had absorbed the sunset over the mountains in southern Arizona, the rainbow sprays of Niagara Falls, and pictures of the Pyramids at Giza.

And she spoke to me, personally. I have never been a fan of pink. I'm more of a brown and green girl. But I had heard that my mother owned a pink Jeep not long before she died, and I thought that was too cool for the room. Anyway, my daughter is also pink. Like tulips. Like cheap neon. Like Mary Kay. Pink. Of course, this is not the only way she and I are polar opposites, though I've been told we are exactly alike. At least, it appears, this is true regarding our attraction to this particular chair.

"Yeah, I've had a lot of interest in that chair. But it's not for sale," Mary Lou exhaled.

"Listen," I heaved, confident like Clint Eastwood, "I have been visiting The Chair for months now. We have developed a relationship. There's Karma involved here." *Go ahead,* I thought, *make my day. Sell me The Chair.*

"I've been thinking I might do a silent auction with some other items not for sale. I'll see if I can organize that, and you can bid on it then," Mary Lou explained.

"Well, I have been visiting her for longer than anyone else, I'm sure. A hundred bucks, right now," I closed assumingly.

"No. Wouldn't be fair," Mary Lou reclosed. "Come back in a couple of weeks." Next time, I would have to hit below the belt. And bring a pack of Kools.

***

Over the next year, I visited The Chair often, sometimes with Cassidy, sometimes not. Sometimes I'd pester Mary Lou, sometimes not. Sometimes she covered her face and ran when she saw me, sometimes not. Sometimes she still offered a silent auction she knew would never come, sometimes not. Sometimes I even thought I should write her a flowery poem about The Chair, sometimes not. Most times I could operate with tact. One time I did not.

I marched in the front door of her store, located Mary Lou, demanded my Chair, and cussed eloquently.

"I'm so tired of dealing with you, Darlene. Take The Damn Chair."

I could not believe my ears. Mother of God, was it true?

"I hope you and your daughter enjoy her as much as I did with my mom back in the day. By the way, I have an incredible pea green sectional, circa 1971, not for sale in the back," Mary Lou purred, tucking my hundred bucks behind a pack of Kools in her front pocket.

Drum Circle

Here, all of us have music falling out of our pockets. We pollute the air with lyrical anarchy. The fire has called us to order; it will preside, judge if our music is truth. If we intend to remain free, we must testify. We must witness for the music.

My friend is the first called. He stands atop the burning stump like a god. As the flames beat the sides of the log, he licks vows off his mandolin. A harmonica hovers somewhere in the smoke. A guitar, a steel drum voice themselves. An ocarina pleads its way out of his pocket to add to his opening statement as the mandolin defends itself throughout the camp. Trills roll off his charred fingertips and articulate emotionally, arguing on a jury of innocent drums. The wheel barrel, the bones on his thigh, finally the fiery stump itself, he commands divinely. Everything is aglow under the spell of his impassioned fingers, pleading insanity.

Vibes now drip off him, sweet honey drawing us to play our defenses, having sworn at least to be honest. A tribe of djembes comes to life, a flute, violin, sitar, conch, tambourine, didgeridoo . . . even my drum, Jack, is vehement. We are syncopated with air and time. We are sharp.

We are major. We resonate in deep dimensions, exhaling song that refuses to be reasoned with. It's torture. None of us is even-keel. No one is calm. We pulsate in the white noise between what is right and everything else. Our victimized fingers submit as the rhythm pummels them into a purple coma. They function only on adrenaline now, the overlying pain resulting in tympanic jubilation, because our song has elevated us beyond time and sanity.

It consumes all space, all sense, every sense. It is logic. Perfection. Intoxicating and sobering. We beat our hands numb to live here in the truth of music, and we can argue nothing further. Without notice, the sun comes up to close the trial, and we sift into slumber, exonerated.

Every fire calls us to testify like this. When winter has coldly sequestered the truth, the music in our pockets burns its way out through our hands.

Old Spice

The day my husband left,
the kids were in diapers,
the condo was in foreclosure,
and 911 had broadened its meaning.
A year later, from a base of concrete steps,
I pulled my grandfather's standard issue WWII bible
from my back pocket,
where it resided when I needed his strong constitution.

Uncle Willie had told me he drank Jack Daniel's with my grandfather.
Wonder if he lived through his old war stories,
or saw his many scars.
Poppy used to make the ship on his chest sail for me,
and I used to dance for him.
And cherry pipe smoke would wander the halls,
Along with his hacking cough.
I watch monster movies by myself now,
but not alone.
And sometimes around Christmas,
the scent of Old Spice finds me,
and a thick safety fills me
the way his smoke had filled our old house.

I hold his bible now, still worn to the shape of
the man he was,
pull from my back pocket
the remains of my marriage in triplicate,
and mount the concrete steps to court by myself,
but not alone.

CHAPTER 2

Celeste A. Turner

Six Ways of Looking at a Feather

I
The squawk of a chicken
screeching early in the morning
means an afternoon of sweeping feathers.

II
Peacock spreads her feathers
like a peaceful rainbow
bursting forth after a cool shower.

III
The gathering of dust
between feather clusters
leaves an image to peek back.

IV
The feather boa covered her bosom
red, radiant and alarming
as if seducing her in plain view.

V
The words of a poem
found their voice
as the feather dipped itself into ink.

VI
If a feather floats by
don't interrupt it's flow.
The journey may have just begun.

Where I Am From

I am from Saturday morning mysteries
Scooby Doo, Shaggy and me covering our eyes
Backyard adventures with mayonnaise jars
Bumble bees buzzing in new glass homes
Quick trips skipping to the corner store
Lingering walks home giggling with friends
Spooky stories and tales on the front porch
Night's arrival announced by streetlights

I am from sliced bananas floating in corn flakes
Better Made potato chips with ketchup on top
Red Pop and fruit-punch decorated lips
Hostess lemon pies, cupcakes, cream filled Twinkies
Smoked beef franks burnt on the grill

I am from 13-hour car rides to Georgia
Eating cold fried chicken in the back seat
Stopping only at gas stations without confederate flags
Greeted by my southern grandma's soft wrinkled hands
Playing with cousins up the hill and down the road

I am from my own little corner being whatever I want to be
Surrounded by *Curious George Flies a Kite, Riding a Bike*
Crayons, pencils and line paper filled with youthful fantasies.
Seeking quiet by pretending to be an only child

I am from 4th of July picnics on an island
Dancing waves at the river's rocky edge
Screaming down a giant slide on potato sacks
The pop, pop, pop of firecrackers
Burst of silver from sparklers burning bright
Gentle breezes of the water under a sunset
Dazzling lights of Canada gazing back at me
Sharing a blanket with my sister and brother

I am from the 67's riots, looting and flames
Neighbors nodding in silence among the fire's soot
Angela Davis shouting, "Black Power, Black Pride"
Black Panther Party fighting for social change
As I listened from the top of winding stairs
Protestors gather resembling my father and uncles

I am from Motown recorded on 45's
Singing *baby, baby* with light bulb microphones
Plucking invisible strings on broomstick guitars
We are *Everyday People*
The opening act for Sly and the Family Stone
Our living room the stage
Momma's *God bless the child that's got his own*
Daddy's *Oh what a night*
Finally going solo in the mirror
As Prince's *Sexy Dancer*
In my first pair of red high heels

I am from big Sunday dinners
Father, Son, Holy Spirit prayers at the table
Homemade vanilla ice cream and butter pound cake
Soaking in rose-petal-scented hot bubble baths
Pillow fights and whispered secrets until lights out
Stories in the dark about the past and the future
Waiting for the Sandman to make my dreams come true

I am from growing up never forgetting
Loving, laughing, living

A Teacher's Guilt

8:00 a.m.

The drive-thru window girl seemed deliberately slow and the coffee advertised HOT would be lukewarm or still boiling in the cup. This didn't stop Terri from waiting anxiously for her turn to place an order of what she called super-unleaded extra caffeine. Caffeine free is a waste of time with the second grade students she has this year. Talkative, shoes off, hollering out answers, and "He has my…" "She won't stop…" were the perfect words to describe the children in Room 223.

The month of May brought out tremendous anxiety, and Terri looked forward to the school year ending. Thoughts of the summer vacation to Cancun, her girlfriends' plan curved the madness that made her feel overwhelmed lately. However, she thought about all the lessons that needed cramming in before the students were promoted June 12. Linda Curry thought $2 + 3 = 4$, Aaron Thomas still struggled with first grade vocabulary, and the last three stories in the reading anthology most likely would not be covered. Terri's apprehension about those students, whom she possibly would have to hold back, resulted in headaches. Along with completing end of the year records and scan sheets for grades, these concerns kept Terri from falling asleep at night and waking up on time in the morning.

Actually, for the past two weeks, Terri practically ran in to the classroom right ahead of her students each morning. Unprofessional? Probably. Could she do better? Maybe. Did she care this particular morning? No! She wouldn't run any red lights getting to school, but doing 50 mph in a 25mph zone could help.

9:00 a.m.

Terri's attendance numbers were getting smaller, and she only had 14 out of 23 today. She hoped that John would be in class on time. Though late most days, he normally arrived before 9:15 a.m. She usually waited until 9:30 to do her student count. At age 7 some of her students had developed what teachers called, "habitual tardiness syndrome." It wasn't their fault. Parents who allow children to awaken at their own leisure were the cause. Didn't they know encouraging these habits at an early age was not good parenting? Never mind that Terri got there some mornings late. As an adult she had consciously decided being on time was overrated.

Remembering the look on John's face, Terri's guilty conscious replayed the words she used on him the day before: "Aren't you tired of always being clueless?" she had snapped. "You can't walk into class late everyday, run your mouth and expect to learn," vaulted off her tongue, leaving a bad taste as soon as the words left her mouth. The techniques she learned during last summer's workshop, Using Non Violent Language in the Classroom, had been forgotten after the twelfth week of school.

Terri liked John. He wasn't a bad child, just a busy one. Unlike some of her other students, he was very street wise for 7 years old. While planning for their Christmas party, he asked if they would play Tunk. "When my mom has a party, they always drink and play cards," John informed the class. When a police officer came for career day, John told him about the gun his cousin kept in the basement. "It's a real gun, but not the kind to kill nobody," John said with a gleeful smile. The officer blew out a disgusted breath giving Terri the impression he didn't have experience talking to small children. She put her hand on John's shoulder and explained that all guns could kill. The officer then went on to share a story about a 5 year old who accidentally shot his brother. Terri knew John witnessed many adult situations but couldn't tell if the officer's stories were making an impact.

Though John was a good reader who enjoyed picture books, math was his best subject, and he could count well beyond the other students. Terri could give him pages of math problems, and he would never take his head up from the desk. Unfortunately for him, he had picked a bad day to play in class. Terri had writing papers to grade and gave the children some independent spelling review to do quietly. She hated calling it, "busy work" because the students were usually busy doing it wrong. John decided "independent" meant do his own thing and began flipping through pages in the back of his workbook, marking a few answers and going to the next page. When Terri finished towering over him, pointing her finger and shouting, John remained quiet the rest of the day.

Though raising her voice at the students did not happen often, Terri felt terrible afterwards. To single out one child plagued her with remorse that attributed to her lack of sleep the night before. The guilt led to a plan that would give her an opportunity to spend some extra time calling on John and using him as a class helper.

There was no reason to think his mother would complain. Students rarely told parents about the occasional shouting a teacher did. They learned early that telling the teacher disciplined them led to the question, "And what were you doing?" Knowing about self-incrimination, telling half the story, and throwing discipline notes away were skills already practiced by second graders.

Just as Terri closed her attendance book, John walked in smiling, showing too many teeth.

"Good morning, Ms. Thomas," he said rushing to his seat. Though he was late most days, it had not yet become a comfortable feeling for him. Terri spent the morning calling on John first to answer questions and ignoring some of his playful behavior.

11:35 a.m.

"I don't know why these children keep shooting at each other," Ms. Lucas said, laying her turkey sandwich and orange from her lunch bag on a red placemat from home. She was considered the National Inquirer of the school and if it was in the news, on the news, or cover of any magazine, she had the inside story and reported as if she had been live on the scene. A social studies teacher for 25 years, she had strong opinions about children, schools and anything else involving education because according to her, "There's nothing new to this game." "I think they should just close school for the rest of the year," she huffed.

Terri tried to avoid these conversations by eating lunch in the second floor teacher's lounge. There they talked about fluff like guests on David Letterman, Oprah episodes they missed, and broken copy machines. However, occasionally Ms. Lucas would grace them with her authoritative opinions: "Two high schools were closed this week because of shootings. Darn shame," Ms. Lucas voice flared.

"I'm glad someone is finally taking notice of what is going on with our children and schools," Terri said. She sat in a chair opposite of Ms. Lucas. "It bothers me that our high schools have become so unsafe."

She laid a stack of spelling papers on the table that needed grading. Her lunch was a diet coke. "I'm glad the counselors are getting involved." Coming from Terri, these statements were startling. Normally these opinions stayed in her head because she didn't want to come off as an instigator.

"Counselors can't help these kids," Ms. Lucas snorted, looking into Terri's eyes. If Lucas' nose flared just a little bit more, she would resemble a bull.

"I guess you think only the police can," Terri rebutted. She knew this would appear to Ms. Lucas as a verbal challenge, and walking away was not her style. Ms. Lucas made no secret about her dislike for the school system she worked within, and most teachers labeled her a complainer stuck in a past life of teaching methods no one practiced anymore.

"This district doesn't have enough counselors to help all these students, and most of them are being laid off," Ms. Lucas said, softening her tone in reaction to Terri's directness.

Some of the other teachers began to focus their attention to the ladies, but dared not speak a word to appear taking sides.

Maybe it was lack of sleep or stress, but Terri could not make her mouth stop, and the words were climbing over each other to come out. "There are a lot of good teachers working with our children…We have some here who are everyday heroes, but they don't show them on the news."

Terri popped the tab on her diet coke can back harder than needed, and in the sudden silence of the room, it sounded like a firecracker. "No one has ever asked me who I thought should be teacher of the year… How can you only choose one teacher from a school district this large and say he or she is the best of the bunch?"

Sweat from the can trickled onto the table, and Terri rubbed the wet puddle with her finger tips like they were a napkin. "There isn't a teacher in this building who would not put themselves in harm's way to save a student in their classroom...I feel bad that the schools are suffering these shootings, but teachers in urban school districts have played psychiatrist and counselor, yet no one ever notices." She gulped down the soda faster than planned, and the quick swallows scratched the back of her throat.

A little out of breath from her rant, Terri realized that the other teachers had begun to eat faster or look toward the window. A few words still clamored at her lips, but she was able to control them.

Ms. Lucas packed up her red nylon lunch bag slowly, one piece at a time.

"Over worked and under paid," she said to the door, turned abruptly to Terri with a worn down gaze, and then left, letting the door close hard.

"Have you looked at this month's Oprah?" another teacher asked, waving the magazine in the air like a ceasefire flag.

Terri felt she had just made real comments in a make-believe conversation that no one cared about. She slowly drank down the rest of her soda but did not feel satisfied.

3:00 p.m.

Terri started calling the children one table at a time to go to their lockers. She did not want to be late to another doctor's appointment. If they were let out on time, and every child was picked up quickly, she would have no problem making the 15-minute drive. Most of her students walked home with older siblings.

Going in the hallway Terri avoided stepping on a blue book bag, several folders, graded papers she had passed back earlier, and a light weight red jacket with black stripes on the floor.

Words began to flare again at the tip of her lips when she felt someone poking her from behind. John shuffled side to side rocking his small body pushing a pack of cherry Now and Later candy in Terri's hand. "This is for you Ms. Thomas," he said with a cheer. "I hope you like that kind."

Terri sensed John's eagerness to win her affections, and the child in her connected that the words she uttered the day before affected him more deeply than she had thought. After all the guilt she felt, John was apologizing and trying to win her over. For a second, she wondered if he originally brought the candy for himself, but this was another opportunity to heal the wound she had created.

Thank you so much, John," she said. "This is my favorite flavor."

She grabbed his small hand and guided him over to the locker hoping, the power of the human touch could act as an eraser for the past. Together they scooped his things off the floor, and he leaned his head slightly on her arm as they walked to where the students were lined up.

3:15 p.m.

After helping John, Terri thought it would be quicker if she grabbed her purse and bag from the classroom after watching the children leave. Her class moved playfully down the hall through the outside doors. Mrs. Johnson, a school aid, leaned against the short chain-link fence as she normally did, oblivious to the pushing and shoving children in front of her. Terri's class had already been warned about wrestling on the grass to avoid anyone getting hurt during dismissal time.

As needed, every child was escorted away, except for John. This was unusual because John's sister, who was a seventh grader from the middle school, was always there with her friends to pick John up first. Terri took a few steps closer to the sidewalk to look for her, instructing John to remain close by Mrs. Johnson's side. A group of older girls had begun to congregate near the large oak tree on the other side of the fence.

Terri debated going over to break up the crowd. Though the majority of them were from the middle school, smaller children began to gather round too.

"Why don't they just go home," Terri said, frowning back at Mrs. Johnson.

"I don't even get involved when it's those big kids," Mrs. Johnson muttered, waving her hands and turning her head in the other direction. It was at this time that Terri realized John had wandered over to the gathering crowd. She zoned in on his red and black jacket, but he had zigzagged into the middle.

"Let's break this up and go home," Terri shouted, walking towards the smaller students. As she put her hands on the back of John's jacket, a tall girl with long black braids slapped another girl so hard John jumped startled and fell back toward Terri. The two girls began grabbing at each others' hair and kicking. Terri yanked one by her arm and the other by the shirt collar. Suddenly, a boy began pushing in the crowd, announcing "Fight over here."

Terri felt herself tumble from the weight of students suddenly being thrust against her. She could see the surprise in John's brown eyes as her head impacted the oak tree. She became dizzy.

8:00 a.m.

Ms. Lucas rolled her window down in the hopes that cool air would fill her nostrils and clear her head. She drove hypnotically on her usual route to school after watching the morning news, hoping there would be some information that the principal had not given her. She normally left the house much earlier because it was her habit to be there 30 minutes prior to the bell every morning. However, 7:45 a.m. flashed in the corner of her television before she grabbed her purse and nylon lunch bag and hurried out the door.

Certainly there would be a story on her car radio news. She listened intently to traffic and weather every 10 minutes which left little time for local news to be reported. Still, Ms. Lucas was hopeful and tried to divide her attention safely between the traffic lights and the radio announcer. Her heart beat faster with each increase in speed and the words Terri spoke the day before played over in her head.

She pulled into the parking lot, and some rock dust blew up into the window. Frustrated, she parked in the shade of one of the landscape trees.

How could such a tragedy happen and no one report the story accurately, she thought to herself, slapping the dashboard with her sweating hand. It would be 85 degrees later, and her heavy body was already tired. The solemn look of another person's face startled her from a car that was already parked. She and Mrs. Johnson met up at the front of her car.

"I cannot believe Terri Thomas lost her life breaking up a fight," Ms. Lucas whispered to Mrs. Johnson as they walked through the school's grey steel back door.

"I saw those kids smash her against the tree, and she slumped to the ground," Mrs. Johnson choked through tears. "I better not see a single one of them outside after school today."

A single tear flowed from Ms. Lucas left eye, but she steadied herself. She did not feel like being the news authority today, but wasn't going to let hallway gossip be the final story. She would also make sure that the principal and school counselor talked to the students in Terri's class.

CHAPTER 3

Holly L. Gilbert-Ryle

A Teacher's View

Brown ones, tans ones
And peach ones too!
Red ones and yellow ones
Just to name a few.
A colorful rainbow of children I see.
Each one looks a little like me!

Day of the Curvaceous Woman

Do you have a hump in your backside bump?
Or arms like small tree trunks?
How about an assorted fruit basket in your front?
Maybe hips that sway with each step you take?
Oh, I know, thighs that remind you of the cake you ate?
If your body Curves at every turn, guess what?
Today is your Celebration Day!
Stand up girls!
Show us those curves!
Be proud of your status piece of art.
Shake it to the left.
Shake it to the right.
Know that you are secretly what most men like!
As Chaka Khans' I'm Every Women falls melodically from the sky
Let your Curvaceous Woman flags fly!

Sassafras Rain

Ploop, Plop, Hmmm, Shhhh
I am life!
My presence is earth's gift from God.
I can nourish or destroy.
Expand mountains or erase existences.
I can cleanse your body of deadly predators' or free your mind of
impure thoughts.
I am summoned by the pounding of Cherokee feet and the silent
wails of Somalian babies.
And when I arrive, I make all things new.
As I land effortlessly on a small blade of grass,
you whisper my name,
Ploop, Plop, Hmmm, Shhhhh.
rain.

The Spice of America

Look at that Bengali girl with her ethnic flare.
Wearing those jeans and gym shoes without a care.
She adds a little spice with her genji and una.

And then there's that Yemeni boy humming that hip hop tune.
Walking with his prayer cloth, so he can pray before noon.

Next there came a Bosnian girl wearing her medallion of gold.
Her I-pod plays the music of her history untold.

Who could miss the African prince walking with his head held high.
Fighting negative stereotypes makes him want to cry.

Then there's the Hispanic beauty swinging her dark hair in sight.
Her hoop earrings sparkle like Hopi Indian Hoop Dancers at night.

The Yemeni girl can't be ignored as she proudly covers her hair.
Her Gucci hijabe is the focus of everyone's stare.

Did you see the girl with cornrows in a beautiful design?
Each design represents her tribe that will always be in her mind.

Oh yeah, there's that good ol' American boy with eyes bright and blue.
His history is embedded in me and you.
The piece of the puzzle that brings the picture into view is…
The Spice of America that is a bit of you and you and you.

Transformation Weekend

My Friday morning began like all the others the past few weeks. Little Amyah began her morning stretches at 5:33am sharp, and one hour to the second, Charles IV; affectionately called C.J., starts the day with a yelping, "Mommy….Mommy…..Mommy where are you?"

"Here I am, Honey!" I answer to the beat of his tiny feet hitting the oak wood floor.

Making list, phone calls and plans, my day began to unfold. Just as I completed the first of eight tasks on my "To Do List," my husband appeared out of the blue with a gleaming smile and a twinkle in his eye.

"Hey let's go to Sassafras for the weekend!"

I glanced at the kids, my "To Do List" and my writing assignments. "How can I go to Sassafras with all of this stuff to do? Besides, it's not in the budget!" My eyes rolled, and my head tilted back at the nerve of his request.

"We are leaving by 3pm. Get some stuff ready for the kid, and I'll pack the car!"

I love an aggressive man! "Whatever you say, Daddy!" I whispered while grabbing diapers, pull-ups and the rest of my daycare supplies. View-Master pictures clicked in my mind of us slow grooving to Marvin Gaye's "Sexual Healing" in a room surrounded by candle light.

Then like a needle screeching across a 45, images of my electric-socket designed hair, yoga pants falling down from C.J. hanging from them like Tarzan swinging to a vine, and Amyah grabbing my right breast like a tipsy chick hogging the mic at karaoke, I yelled into the baby monitor, "This is insane. We can't go 700 miles with these passengers!"

I fell on the floor and kicked in the air, lamenting my past romantic life. C.J. looked at me with his marble brown eyes as if he were seeing a stranger. "What's wrong, Mama?" Guilt quickly overcame me before

I could answer. What kind of mother am I, using my babies as an excuse for my inability to be spontaneous? "Daddy wants to go to the mountains!"

"The mountains?" he echoed with his nose scrunched up trying to picture mountains.

"Yes the mountains, but Mama doesn't think it's a good idea!"

"Mama, what is mountain?"

Just then it hit me, I started to pack again. C.J. watched with a confused stare. "Mama you go to mountain?" "Nope, we are going to see the mountains!" A smile riddled with dimples and jelly from breakfast spread across his face. "Yay mountains!"

Moments earlier a voice whispered to me, "Go. You must go!" The voice wouldn't accept any excuses I had to offer. It just kept saying, "Go!" As I committed to this whimsical request of my husband, I began to overflow with excitement at the thought of C.J. seeing a mountain.

Shoes

I believe the soles of each pair of shoes gives you a glimpse of the soul wearing the shoes, and here is my story.........

Big Mama loved a good pair of pumps! She worked in them, went to church in them and marched for equality in them too!

I loved to play in my Big Mama's shoes. The last time I slipped my size 5 in her size 10 black leather pumps, something magical happened. Her soul leaped out from the sole of those shoes, and I never viewed Big Mama the same. As I admired the shoes, a transformation took place. I began to hear voices of children playing tag and Big Mama yelling, "I'm gonna get my switch if you don't get down out that tree, Darlene!"

Flashes of light illuminated shadows of her on her knees scrubbing floors in those shoes. When I wiggled my toes inside them, hums of "We Shall Overcome," resonated in the room. My insides began to tremble and with each step I took, more scenes from her life began to unfold. Involuntary movements of my body parts acted out each episode.

I marched around the room with a picket sign chanting, "Equality for all!" I fell to my knees weeping as reflections of Martin, Medgar and Malcolm flashed before me! My chest inflated with patriotism as I witnessed the return of a battered son from Vietnam.

Then suddenly, I spun around with my arms stretched, dancing with the Holy Ghost, as Big Mama sang, "Amazing Grace…." Stumbling right into Big Mama's dresser with the large square mirror, I looked up and saw me. The offspring of a pair of pumps with worn down heels and weathered soles were still clean and shined to perfection.

CHAPTER 4
Mary Cox

Celebrate the Moment

Celebrate the moment;
Grab the seconds; Hang on to the warmth;
Build your life with these instances of wonder:
Each rainbow reflected in the eye of a lover,
Each rain drop that soothes away pain,
Each flower that blossoms with hope.
These are the moments of celebration.

Selene

Selene drifts in heavenly gossamer
Trailing a veil of light
The weight of the light
Caresses the world below.

Unlike her brother
Who drives our lives,
Selene calms us
And offers peace.

Selene drifts in heavenly gossamer
Trailing a veil of light
The veil passing over us
Erases the errors of the day.

The Garden

The smell of sauerkraut, cabbage rolls, and boiled cabbage filled the halls and snuck under the door. She pictured heads of cabbage boiling in large vats, like baby heads bouncing and bubbling. She felt the bile rise in her throat. The smell was making her sick. She leaned her head out the open window hoping to get a whiff of clear air; instead she was slapped with the heat rising from below. The smell of rotting garbage, horse droppings and melting tar were hardly a relief from the inside smell of cabbage.

Grace rested her chin on her folded hands, hands that were red and cracked from the hot water at the laundry where she worked. Soon she would have to leave for her job—-the hot steam, scalding water, heavy sheets, the smell of bleach pricking her nose, other people's laundry, other people's lives.

She often dreamed what life outside of this tenement would be like. There would be no shrill calls in languages she did not understand, no sad plants in pots trying to find the sun as it danced between buildings. She felt like the sad flowers, pale, tired, thirsty for a better life. But it would never come—-no one would rescue the flower and no one would rescue her.

Her man had left to search for freedom in the Alaskan gold fields only to meet death at the poker table, or so the letter had said. Now after two months, all that stretched before her were long days of toil and hard work, living in dank smelling rooms.

She climbed out on the fire escape. Her mother had always forbidden it. She said it was not lady-like to let people perhaps see up her skirt. Self-consciously she wrapped her ankle length skirt tighter about her legs as she climbed up to the roof.

As her head cleared the low wall of the roof and she reached to pull herself up, she came to a stop. Spread before her were an amazing number of tubs and pots full of flowers of all colors and sizes. She sat on the wall and swung her feet over onto the roof. She wandered between the pots, her hand touching the soft petals. The dusty smell of lavender surrounded her. Tiny meadows of nodding daisies beckoned her on. A thorn of a rose bush grabbed at her skirt begging to be noticed. Tall spikes of gladiolas stood at attention wearing buttons of red and yellow, pink and white. Small pots of thyme and rosemary and basil huddled together mixing their leaves and elixirs.

She sat on a bench between two large tubs of geraniums. Their acrid scent proved she was not dreaming. First a contented sigh, then a laugh erupted from deep in her soul. From where she sat she could see the ocean.

A movement caught her eye and she turned. Grace saw a woman bending over a tub of lavender. Placing her hands on the small of her back, making a soft oomph, the woman straightened. When she turned, she started at seeing Grace. Her ancient face broke into a smile deepening the creases on either side of her mouth, causing the eyes to become slits in the wrinkled face.

Grace gestured to the surrounding tubs and looked questioningly at the dwarf of a woman. She nodded proudly and slowly shuffled over to Grace's bench.

"Witaj, kim jesteś?" she asked. While Grace's accent marked her as an immigrant, she spoke no other language than English. She smiled, held out her hands palms up and shook her head.

Undeterred, the woman sat next to her. The woman pointed to her ring finger. "Żonaty?" she asked.

Assuming she understood the question, she shook her head, "Dead" she said, "Gone."

The woman smiled and stared straight ahead. They sat in companionable silence for a while. Suddenly Grace realized it was late; she needed to go to work. She turned to her companion planning to pantomime leaving when the woman reached over and laid her hand on Grace's abdomen. "Kiedy?" she asked.

Confused, Grace tried to move away, but the old woman's hand remained. She gave Grace a wistful smile, "Czy chcesz chłopiec i dziewczynka?"

As the old woman patted softly, Grace felt the quickening. Her mind ran in several directions, counting days and weeks, moods and restlessness, smells that made her sick. She looked at the old woman, her eyes wide with comprehension. The woman smiled and nodded, "Tak, tak."

Tears filled Grace's eyes—tears of joy, tears of fear—she was not sure. The old woman leaned over and kissed Grace on the cheek. "Powodzenia. Przyjdź i często odwiedź ogrodzie." Grace merely nodded, understanding only the intent, not the words.

The old woman left walking to the stairway door. Grace sat for a while. She thought about what this would mean to her life. How would she manage? She was not sure, but when she rose and lowered herself down the fire escape, she moved as if carrying a gift of great value.

It was perhaps the surreal feelings of her recent discovery that made it so easy for her accept the presence those familiar arms that awaited her and helped her off the fire escape.

CHAPTER 5

Ellen Kinsley

Monologue of the Bumblebee

I am busy! Go away!
Don't shade the light from me,
Pitiful human son!
I am in charge of life…
Don't you smell and see the amber golden drops?
Lucid petals of the naughty rose?
Smoothness of the pearly butterfly?
Harmony of the linden clusters?
Home of the forest badgers?
If not, go away, pitiful human son!

Alphabetical Poem

Ammunition bangs…
Conditions decoy…
Enigma flamboyantly glimmers…
Heal.
Instance jerks kings.
Lapses mistreat…
Notions occur partially.
Quick rays saturate tales…
Unbiased vim waves experience.
Youthful zenith…

Magic of the Childhood

Many years ago in the realm of the 6 year old
There were serene summer evenings,
Simple swing under the apple tree branch,
Bitter amber sap on the apricot bark,
Softly golden sunsets, chattering birds,
Smell of old wooden fence,
Yarn of years was endless…

Where I am From…

I am from my father's sandy town
Framed with mountain ash trees.
I am from blackberries with cottage cheese
Served on the heavy oak table,
From iron cast pans full of tasty wild mushrooms.

From fields of forest strawberries I am…
I came in May from blooming woods
I am from spring but born in February…

I am from magazines "Around the World"
With articles from *National Geographic*
I am from travels, travelers, and nature…
I am from past, but I will continue.

My Bits

Thanksgiving is waiting for us…
Universe is ready for the winter.
Reign of darkness outside…
Amber candles on my table,
Smell of wax and honey…
Red and orange dance of flame
Life and future are together.

Slavic Haiku

The crescent is a pearl tooth of my baby
Smiling at us from the heaven.
The sun is a face of my baby
Looking at us from the heaven.
The summer soft rain is the mood of my baby
Covering us with happiness.
A song of a sad-sweet bird in September
Makes my soul feel autumn.

Seven-Words Poem

Sweet rosehips in the chime of the evening breeze
give me the fragrance of life.
Lily is jealous because her petals are blurry
under the moss of a pine.
Lapis lazuli sky gently rocks
the transparent dragonfly.

Halloween

Halo around the moon…
All people are enchanted.
Lullaby is sifting from the window…
Lunar pebbles on the roof…
Opal shadows on the curtain…
Wiry witches levitating above the town…
Empty house on the hill,
Eerie air all around…
Narrow leaves are twirling on the streets…
Night is reigning everywhere…

Darlene's Place

I like nature. I cannot stay indoors. I have to walk on the grass, feel dew on my skin, smell rainbows of flowers, and see the depths of the skies. I am melting in the rays of the velvety sun. Bees keep working on clover honey, black raspberries lure me, and mulberry is on the guard of the apple trees. Light indigo morning glory talks its shade and hue to green vines. Peacefulness of July morning is solemn. Celebration of the yarn of life is without end.

My Bedroom

My bedroom… Small, without a door, shared with my grandfather. Old, mahogany-chestnut color wardrobe trunk with smell of old times, with sharp voice of the opening drawers—always contented a well-known surprise for me: a Japanese bamboo umbrella, Chinese ladies' sweaters touched by moths, embroidered towels from India, skirts with fancy buttons, and certain documents which were untouchable for everyone except my grandfather.

I vividly picture the sunny late afternoon window, perpetual beams of light, breezy, frisky shadows on the lacy curtain. The huge mulberry tree had given freely the shapes of its branches and leaves to the light wind that was throwing them nonchalantly to the window; and again—the sense of infinite time caught in the peace of that window.

South - East Ukraine... The late 1960s...

Hot, dusty summers. There was no rain in these times—I remember. Small town of miners and peasants: rich, poor, drunk, hardworking, playing cards, singing, buying and selling fresh gardens' produce at the street market. Mix of the dialects and languages.

There was a part of the town, right behind our backyard, called Shanghai. Forbidden place. No kids were allowed to set foot over there. I did. What a pleasure it was to run, climb the steep ravines with prickly vegetation, play with gypsy children that had tepid palms of the hands; to make friends, and inhale the air of my native steppes. And there was a mysterious incomprehensible attraction, a huge old cemetery with wooden crosses, bleak photographs, faded artificial flowers, and marble and granite tombstones. The cemetery was situated on the top of the several hills. The majestic view of the town lying beneath and around you in the lavender haze of the pre-evening hours was captivating enough to make a double trip every day.

I loved my routes to Shanghai and the cemetery. Then I hurried home to the cozy warmth of the kitchen, ate supper with my grandfather, and savored my secret, my mystic attraction.

Shoes

These shoes take me to the recent past of my country when it was under the iron rule of the "steel" man Stalin. He was creating the inescapable web of labor camps for all free thinking people, for all suspicious, in his belief, citizens.

The conditions over there were inhuman: all women and men had to work from dawn to dusk, wearing rough, very often oversized shoes and clothes; they experienced lack of food, absence of medical care, and humiliation. The inmates (that's how they were addressed) were accused of being traitors, spies, and just dangerous elements for the Soviet Union. Millions of them perished in the vast forests of Siberia and Northwest Territories of Russia.

This picture reminds me of my grandparents who lived through this ordeal and who had been removed from their native village in sunny Ukraine and were sent in cattle cars for to the North areas near the White Sea. In spite of everything, they survived, but had lost their babies. That's why I do not have my uncle and my aunt.

Big, clumsy, and old shoes on the dirt—the symbol of torture, dictatorship, and lost lives. The symbol for all human kind: People, be watchful!

CHAPTER 6

Mary Beth Revesz

The Balcony Chronicles

There are places that exist where you can find magic every time you step in its realm. These places are magical not because of how they are decorated or how expensive it costs to travel to them, but because you find them and the experiences you have there transcend everyday life to form the memories of your heart.

There are many special places like this in my life, but I have been thinking about a certain one. It is a place where the bonds of friendship, family and true love were forged. It is a simple balcony at the apartment I lived in when I was in my late twenties and early thirties.

To me this apartment was perfect. It was nestled on a tree-lined street a few minutes away from the hubbub that was Downtown Royal Oak. There was a tiny kitchen with black and white tile and appliances that some might call old and worn, but I call vintage and retro. The kitchen led to a large room that served as a dining room and living room. Off to the side was a small nook that served as a little office; in the other direction was a hallway that led to the bathroom and then to two bedrooms. The larger bedroom belonged to my roommate, Christina, and the smaller bedroom belonged to me.

My bedroom had a door that led to the enchanted balcony. The balcony floor was constructed of roof shingles and covered with industrial strength outdoor carpeting. There was a railing of iron bars that enclosed the balcony. Overhead was a metal overhang that protected anyone from getting a sunburn. The view was our driveway and the apartment building beyond a wooden fence. It's not particularly picturesque or pastoral.

But this is where the magic would happen, and it started with a table...

Volume 1: The Table

Sometimes a roommate is just a roommate. Erin, whose taste was so completely different than mine it was if an imaginary line were drawn down the middle of our freshman dorm room; Becky, whose clutter threatened to overtake our shared space; and Liz, whose moods I had to carefully gauge before I walked into the room. Their presence was brief yet meaningful, but they have drifted off into the periphery of my life.

But there have been others who have been much more than a roommate. Kelly is one. She was my roommate my sophomore and senior years in college, and she will definitely get her own set of chronicles one day.

Then there is Christina. It is her apartment that belongs to the balcony. When I moved into her upper flat in 2002, we were former colleagues who had hung out and had fun together. We connected with each other through music. Both of us had mad love for Neil Finn and the same favorite Smiths song, "There is a Light that Never Goes Out." It was serendipity that brought us together. Her roommate had bought a house and was moving out a week after my lease was up. I had been living by myself for a year, and was ready to share living expenses with someone again.

I had moved in on a warm July day, and after about a week, Christina's old roommate had cleared her stuff out. We were standing on the balcony and realized it was missing something. We had a few stools that Christina had purchased at IKEA. There were some nice hanging plants and some flowers in pots. We even had wind chimes.

Christina said to me, "We need a table."

"We definitely need a table," was my response.

And we stood there for a while pondering what kind of table we could buy. A patio table would probably be too big for the balcony, and a card table did not have functional flair.

"Inspiration will strike us. We'll find the perfect table." I said.

A few days later, we decided to walk downtown to visit the farmer's market. We started heading down Washington Avenue, talking about our week, and planning our vegetable purchases at the market.

There it was—sitting on the edge of the curb, turned on its side with a sign taped to its front with the words "$40 or best offer" hastily scribbled in black marker. Made of metal with a beige laminate top, it was yellow, the color of mustard and sunshine. Although covered in a layer of grime and dirt, it was the perfect size and the perfect complement to our balcony dreams.

We both stood there looking at the table, smiling. We turned to each other.

"That is our table," Christina smiled.

"That is so 100 percent completely our table." I responded.

We walked up to the house and knocked on the door. While we waited for a response, we pooled our money together, twenty-five dollars. Hopefully this can be a best offer. The door opened to reveal an older woman dressed in a housecoat with a cigarette between her fingers and a voice that intimated this had not been her first smoke.

"What do you want?" she growled.

Christina took the lead, "We'd like to make an offer on the table. Would you take 25 dollars?"

We waited as she took a drag on her cigarette. She sighed, "I was really hoping for 40."

Christina and I looked at each other. "If you'll take 25 we can get it off your hands right now," she said hopefully.

"I really think I can get $40." Obviously, we were dealing with a grizzled veteran of many a garage sale and bartering session. I knitted my brows together and said to our foe, "You have it out on the curb. Somebody could just come and take it in the middle of the night. With us, you can get 25 bucks right now." I crossed my arms in a show of determination. It was now a matter of pride for us to get that table. And to get it for 25 dollars.

The lady knew she had lost. "What the heck, you two look like sweet girls. All right. Just get it out of here as soon as possible."

We handed over the money and she closed the door. As the door shut, we jumped up and down in excitement over our victory.

The farmer's market a distant memory, Christina sat on the curb guarding our prize while I ran to get my Chevy Blazer to bring our table home. I pulled up alongside the curb. It was then we realized that getting this table onto our balcony was not going to be easy.

For one, it was very top heavy and very awkward to move. After several tries, we finally got it up and in the back of the Blazer. Problem two, it didn't fit all the way into the back of the truck. We didn't have anything to tie it down, so Christina sat in my backseat and held on to two of its legs as I drove down Washington to Catalpa at about ten miles an hour. Luckily, it was a short trip. When we got to our apartment, we faced an even bigger obstacle: getting it up the stairs, into our apartment and onto the balcony.

We lugged the table out of my car and awkwardly got it up on the porch. I adjusted the screen door it so that it stayed propped open. Christina and I each grabbed a side of the table, looked to see if we could maneuver it through the door, and realized there is no chance that it will fit. Still, we tried it anyway, thinking the forces that brought this table into our lives would grant one more wish. No dice.

Our next idea was to flip it over. We got it upside down after much consternation and one squished toe, grasped two legs each and lifted the table with hope springing eternal. Still no luck.

We finally found success by turning the table on its side and getting one end of the table in the door and then swinging it sideways to get the other end inside. We slapped each a high-five only to realize we still needed to get it up the stairs. Our heads and hearts sunk with frustration, but we had gritted our teeth, determined to have our table in its rightful place. We had hit on the right strategy. The only way it would get up the stairway would be on its side. So we went to work, getting to the second floor, step by step. It took several attempts through fits of laughter, and Christina nearly got flattened as my hand slipped, but we finally made it. Slowly but surely we got it through the front door to our apartment and down the hallway, and finally, gratefully, out onto the balcony.

We spent the next hour scrubbing it clean, giggling over the misadventures of the morning and making plans for grand dinners eaten alfresco, when Christina suddenly had an idea.

"I'll be right back." And she was off down the stairs, out of the apartment and into her car. She had been gone for about 15 minutes when her car returned. She got out, holding a bag from the hardware store.

She came out onto the balcony with the bag. It was spray paint, but it was a special kind of spray paint that turned the boring beige laminate into a chalkboard table top. Now our table was perfect, and had the added bonus of being an actual written record of what was going on our mind that day.

So sometimes a roommate is just a roommate, someone you let go in the shower first and for whom you take phone messages. Sometimes, however, a roommate becomes a lifelong friend. And all it really took was moving a table. Our friendship was forged that day through the trials and tribulations of getting that table onto our balcony, and it was strengthened by the dinners eaten on that table, the hangman and Yahtzee games, the glasses of wine that we drank as we discussed life and made lists of our dreams and accomplishments. One of those lists changed my life forever.

Volume 2: The List

It was a Friday night early in September, when I wasn't too exhausted from stresses of the classroom to enjoy one of those alfresco dinners out on the balcony. Christina was there, and so was my friend Kelly. There was much laughter, and talk soon turned to the future. As we talked, we each made lists of dreams and aspirations we have for the future. My list looked something like this:

1. Travel to Greece
2. See Bruce Springsteen in concert
3. Join a gym.
4. Take cooking lessons

All in all, a pretty good list, I thought, and I left it there as a record of my thoughts.

The next day, my brother Mark and his wife Jami came over for a visit. It was a perfectly sunny Saturday, and I was looking forward to walking into town and getting some lunch. Jami and Mark had been married the previous November, and I was still getting used to the idea that someone actually married my brother.

They arrived and soon we were out on the balcony, and I was showing them my list. Jami smiled and said, "Give me the chalk. I've got something to add to the list."

I hesitated for a moment. Jami and I get along great, but she can be blunt and I can be sensitive, and sometimes I let my feelings get all out of whack with some of her "friendly advice." Still, I handed the chalk over and braced myself for what she was going to write.

First, she wrote the number 5, and then "a b" followed by "a u" and "a y." Next, came the word "baby." The final word was "clothes." Then she turned back to me with a grin on her face, as she let the words sink in. However, I wasn't cooperating. I was confused.

"What? Why would I need to buy baby clothes?"

"DUHHHH!" Jami and Mark rolled their eyes in unison at my confusion.

Then slowly, but surely the synapses fired in my brain, and what they were trying to tell me became completely clear. I was going to be an aunt! I WAS GOING TO BE AN AUNT!!!! Emotions overwhelmed me at that moment! Happiness and utter joy, as well as concern and surprise. We celebrated with lunch at Zumba's, and the pregnancy progressed with few complications. Mark Edward, Jr. was born the following May after a marathon labor (he is a stubborn one), and my niece Andi Ida came a year later.

And since that day on the balcony, my personal to-do list has never been the same. I know that being an aunt is not the same as being a parent, but it is a responsibility I take very seriously. Instead of traveling to Greece, we travel to the library and Chuck E. Cheese, and even going to Target becomes an adventure. I have seen Bruce Springsteen in concert since then, but I also know songs by the Backyardigans and Thomas the Tank Engine. I go to the gym, but I enjoy the exercise I get from playing hide and seek at the park even more. Cooking is limited to Macaroni and Cheese rather dishes with rich and savory ingredients. Best of all, Marky and Andi are the kind of kids that I would hope they would be: smart, funny, creative. And I am their favorite aunt.

Looking back on that day, finding out that I was going to be an aunt had to happen on that balcony. It's a much better story than if Mark and Jami just told me in the kitchen or somewhere else in the apartment. There are so many happy memories of good times on that balcony. However, some are bittersweet. I am happy with how this next one turns out, but when it starts one cold winter week, I am actually annoyed to be standing on the balcony....

Volume 3: The Beginning of the End

It was the last week in January, and I am wrapped in my winter coat and a blanket. I am sitting on a stool on our balcony. It is nighttime and it is bitterly cold. This was the third day that week I have come out here to keep Christina company, and I am starting to get annoyed. It is too cold to be here. As beautiful as the balcony is in the summertime, it is bleak in the winter. Our plants are dead, and the hanging baskets swing empty in the bitter wind. The night is crystal clear, and the wind chill hovers precipitously at the zero mark.

We were watching Christina's car. It hadn't worked since Sunday. If I were her, I would have gone straight to the dealership and that would be that. But Christina's not me and she had a plan. She called Steve, a friend of a friend, to come over and fix it. He is an engineer, and likes to work on cars. Christina told me he does all his own oil changes, and spark plug replacements, and even rotates his own tires. I was impressed coming from a family who are challenged in finding the gas cap on their cars. He came over Sunday night to work on it. And Monday night. And Tuesday night. And now it's Wednesday. I began to wonder if he's not as cool with cars as he thinks he is.

So there we were shivering on the balcony as he worked on the car in the glow of the security light from the apartment building that sat behind us. And while I didn't realize it then, it is the beginning of the end of our time on the balcony.

Because Steve does know how to fix cars. But dragging out a complicated repair for days is his way of getting to spend time with Christina, and Christina doesn't really care that it took him a week to fix her car because she got to spend time with Steve. By the time the car is finally fixed, Steve and Christina were a couple. And then he began spending just as much time on our balcony as we did.

Two years passed. I was sitting on the balcony reading. It was Memorial Day weekend, and the sky was blue and perfect. Christina just returned from a camping trip with Steve, and she is positively beaming.

"He did it."

I didn't have to guess what "it" was. She held out her hand for me to see the sparkling diamond on her ring finger.

"Well, it's about time. I was beginning to get upset that he was dragging his feet," I said as I gave her a big hug. Soon after they put a down payment on a house on 2.5 acres in Ann Arbor.

Since our lease was up in a few months, I briefly considered keeping the apartment by myself. But I was also considering leaving my job, and not knowing where I was going to end up, moving back to Trenton seemed the most logical plan.

As July and the end of our lease came, we were faced with a dilemma. What to do with our chalkboard table? It had started to show signs of wear: the slate was chipping and it wobbled; yet it was the place where so many memories were set. I had moved my belongings a few weeks before, and Christina had slowly moved her things to her new house, but the table lingered in our thoughts.

The table had belonged to both of us. It wouldn't be right for one of us to have it. So in the end, we decided to move it out and leave it on the curb for someone else to claim as their own. Funnily enough, it was a lot easier to move it out than it was to move it in, and as we got it to the curb, and placed a sign that said "FREE" in block letters on its slate tabletop, we couldn't help but feel a little sentimental. Sure enough it was gone by the next morning. I don't know its new owner, but I hope they treated that table well. I hope there were many happy memories at that table.

I happened to be in Royal Oak recently, and I was beckoned by "the good old days" to drive by the old apartment. It looked vacant, and I couldn't bear to pull in the driveway to see the balcony. I didn't want to see it empty and bleak with no flowers growing in hanging baskets, no yellow table, no celebrations. Instead, I choose to search for my own balcony, where I can feel as happy and content as I did back then. I'll know it when I see it.

CHAPTER 7
Arthur Orme

William Wordsworth

Poetic Justice

Two days after being notified he was still grumbling to himself as he entered the classroom where thirty students were seated at old oak tables with blank expressions and pencils poised to record every word which dripped caustically from his lips.

"Anybody know any filthy limericks?" he growled. But his boat seemed launched on a sea of silent and empty faces with no wind for the sails.

"Well, it doesn't matter. Anyone know what a limerick is?" Still no response. It was difficult to make waves in shallow water.

"How about a Haiku?" Once again there was no response.

"A sonnet?...an Ode?" Nothing.

"Anyone ever hear of Shakespeare? Milton? Wordsworth? Keats?" he pleaded. Still they only watched.

"Is anyone alive out there? Anyone know any good song lyrics?" At last a hand went up.

"I know 'Killing me softly with his songs,'" a rather wistful sorority type ventured timidly.

"Well then," he smiled, somewhat relieved. "That is indeed something. That's a start anyway. That particular phrase provides us with an example of one device used in poetry called figurative language."

Another hand shot up.

"Yes, Miss...

"Dixon sir, Tracy Dixon..."

"But don't call me sir," he interrupted. "I may seem old from your perspective, but I'm not that old from mine...not even as old as poetry... Dr Shelburn will do...But proceed. You were saying?"

The young girl in the somber colored sweater and wire rimmed glasses responded: "I don't get it. It don't make any sense. Songs don't kill."

"It doesn't make sense, exactly....exactly....precisely the point, now we're getting somewhere," he warmed, feeling the wind in his sails; and he was about to launch into the realms of metaphor when he realized she was still talking.

"But there are things that kill softly," she continued enthusiastically, without the slightest inhibitions, "...A slit throat just below the voicebox works or smothering with a pillow when the person's asleep... Some kinds of poisons are undetectable too..."

"Dear God," Shelburn groaned to himself.

"I think songwriters tend to avoid reality and hard facts by hiding behind pretty words," she concluded.

Through years of practice Shelburn had learned to recover his composure quickly.

"Ah, yes... yes, ah, I suppose they do. But I'm sure you'll find true poetry more to your liking in those regards. In any case, that's precisely the point I was making...that songs don't really kill, not literally. It's a figure of speech. Poetry frequently uses such language that is figurative rather than literal. Does anyone know why?" Again there was a silent abyss to be bridged.

The cynical thought occured to him that if he said "the world will end tomorrow," they might all dutifully write it down without expressing any interest or concern.

"Anyone care to guess?" he ventured again.

"To hide the truth so that people won't find out?" Tracy asked.

"Well, ah, not exactly. It's more to create layers of meaning and ambiguities, to develop themes in symbolic and picturesque ways."

"Oh, I get it. Like a red herring or a smokescreen to disguise the crime." She seemed very satisfied with her explanation. Shelburn could see it was going to be a very long semester.

"The world is too much with us," he mumbled. "Why don't we try another approach," he announced as he scrawled on the blackboard the words "Westward wind when wilt thou blow?" He made a few comments about Elizabethan ballad style, but the remainder of the class period was no more successful than its beginnings.

Shelburn walked wearily back to his office lamenting the quality of modern students, and slumped into his chair. Maybe he should consider retirement after all. "They're not interested in anything that's not contemporary or job related," he mumbled to himself..."Have to spoon feed everything. It's all the fault of computers. Kids today have lost any sense of discovery, inquiry, creativity, investigation—all gone—all sadly gone. They think all the answers are preprogramed. Life is one big computer game. Just feed the right commands, push a few buttons and solutions magically appear on the screen. Heaven forbid they should be required to think about something or investigate, or build anything from scratch... The marvel of the age," he scoffed. It was the very same marvel that had not been programmed to notify the new teaching assistants of their assignments, making it necessary for tenured professors to teach the 200 level courses for nonmajors.

His enrollment list arrived later that morning, computer generated and late as usual. The admissions-class assignment beauracracy had, according to Dr. Shelburn, long since become "too complex to be comprehendable, let alone functional." His eyes scanned over the top of his glasses at the list of names and majors; packaging, advertising, communications (now there was a possibility worth cultivating), psychology, education, political theory, marketing, apparel design- what kind of a major was that! At the bottom of the page was a late addition not in alphabetical sequence; "Tracy Dixon, criminal justice." The sinking feeling took hold once again. "Oh dear, I might have guessed," he thought. He felt a migrain returning and found in his top drawer the bottle of aspirin which had been a constant consolation and comfort in a changing academic environment. He picked up his pipe, the one he was no longer allowed to smoke indoors, for security; but he was unable to erase the Shakespeare sonnet haunting his mind:

"That time of life thou mayst in me behold,
when yellow leaves or few or none do hang
upon those boughs which shake against the cold."

It was indeed a tedious task, filled with the hauntingly vacant expressions of students appropriately designated by Shelburn as "the class of the living dead." Students who, according to Shelburn would, perhaps by spring thaw, have no greater appreciation of the poetic sublime than when they started, had all miraculously converged on one spot and presented themselves as ghostly apparitions regularly three times a week since the beginning of semester.

By midterm Shelburn's aspirins were gone, and he made a mental note to certainly buy a larger bottle, industrial strength if possible, before embarking on the sobering reality of grading final papers. Elizabeth, the blond (although, Shelburn preferred the term "light headed") communications major, proved to be more interested in social communication than the literary variety. The one with the shaved head; Ted Chiropodus, had come under the spell of Krishna and was convinced that the greatest poetry was the meditative "om." Will, the journalism major, had developed an interest in Edgar Guest which seemed at least something, a beginning albeit perhaps an ignominious one. Tracy was certainly the most outspoken and lively of the group. Yet it was not without a small amount of apprehensive trepidation that Shelburn acknowledged her upraised hand. "Was Keats's Grecian Urn a burial urn?...Who 's ashes were inside?"

Shelburn dexterously side stepped the issue by pointing out that Keats himself had said "Beauty is truth and truth beauty" and that was ALL we needed to know. Still he could surmise behind Tracy's penetrating eyes lingering doubts. She suspected foul play. What did Keats have to hide by diverting attention with such a trite platitude? To Tracy it seemed a Romantic blindness in Shelburn not to address such obvious red herrings and be curious about the hard core seemy reality lurking just under the surface. On the other hand, Tracy always had something to say and at those times when the communal conspiracy of silence confronted the simplest of Shelburn's questions, the blessing of an opinion in itself was enough to calm the aging professor's fears.

But when she subsequently ventured her opinion that Keats was wrong; that beauty was anything but true- just a superficial smokescreen to conceal the hard facts, Shelburn realized that he was face to face with a hardboiled skeptical cynicism which rivalled only his own in its universal application.

"Such a refreshingly pleasant sense of the morbid," he reflected as he walked home later that afternoon. A smile came naturally, and for a brief moment he was afraid of cracking the Charles Bronson persona on such an overcast Michigan day with no shadow to reinforce his tough, hard-boiled self image.

The semester plodded on and on and so did Shelburn. But with soggy galoshes and a sack lunch, the hard line approach seemed increasingly out of place. His herringbone jacket was beginning to fray at the cuffs. The elbows were worn dispite the leather patches.

As midterm passed into early May it was a time for rejoicing and for assigning final papers upon which grades would be based. It was the best of times. It was the time, according to Shelburn to arrive at the very heart of the matter: the matter, of course, being Romanticism. "Ah, Romanticism." It was a time for Wordsworth's Lucy poems; a time to dispense with Neoclassic satire, Elizabethan sonnets and Imagism to return to the real rapture. And so he introduced the glorious Lucy poems by writing on the board, "A slumber did my spirit seal."

"And what does that mean?" he asked.

"Could mean going to sleep gave him an attitude," Ted cracked.

"Yes indeed it could," Shelburn beamed, "But unfortunately it doesn't," he glared over his glasses. Refusing to become discouraged, he offered clues. By now the entire poem was before them.

A slumber did my spirit seal;
I had no human fears.
She seemed a thing that could not feel
The touch of earthly years.

No motion has she now, no force;
She neither hears, nor sees;
Rolled round in earth's diurnal course,
With rocks, and stones, and trees.

"Sleep is often used to refer to death," he hinted hopefully.

"Is it about being depressed about someone dying?" Elizabeth asked.

"Bingo," Shelburn bubbled, "good work...most perceptive."

"But how do we know that?" Tracy's voice interrupted.

Shelburn, who couldn't see how it could be otherwise, was dumbfounded. "Why, because that's what the words say...a slumber, or a death, sealed my spirit." Shelburns boat of enthusiasm had sprung a leak.

"But couldn't it also mean my spirit sealed a slumber? Couldn't it? I mean, there isn't any punctuation or anything." She pointed out with confidence.

"Well... I suppose it could...he thought, but what would that mean? It would be nonsense wouldn't it? He had no sooner uttered the words when the possibilities began to dawn, and his mouth dropped open. "What exactly are you getting at Miss Dixon?" Although spoken with slow deliberation and seeming coolness, nothing could stop the heat he felt behind the collar.

"Did someone kill Lucy, Dr. Shelburn?"

"Of course not," Shelburn laughed. It's just a poem about the loss of a loved one and the resulting grief. There probably never was a real Lucy, you know. Hartman, that is Herbert Hartman claims the name is a standard fictional name used in many of the elegiac works of the period. What would make you think someone killed Lucy?"

"The poem does. It gives me the creeps. It's almost like a confession note written by a psychopath. He claims he sealed a slumber, and he's not likely to be brought to justice."

Shelburn kept telling himself to remain composed, but the anger was building. "Wordsworth was hardly a psychopath," he resumed. Think about it for a moment that is about the numbness and grief; the indifference to joy which results from the loss of a loved one. What better way of saying it: 'A slumber did my spirit seal'. Can you all see how we arrive at that?" The question was met with the usual sea of tranquility, so he continued. "How about you, Miss Dixon, do you see how we arrived at this?"

Not wanting to make a scene, she differed to his authority. "Oh, now that you explained it , it sorta makes sense."

"Wonderful." But he could tell she wasn't totally convinced, and something in her noncommittal answer seemed disconcerting.

Later, during office hours, Tracy appeared at the door, notebook in hand. " Why Miss Dixon" he brightened, "please come in... sit down."

"I wanted to talk to you about this Lucy case." She sat down pencil in hand. " I've been looking at some of the other poems, and I think I see some of that poetic ambiguity you were telling us about. That is, I still see some criminal suggestions here, and I think I'd like to investigate the case further for my final paper."

"Indeed, well, I daresay I don't think you'll find much. Wordsworth, after all, was a most respected poet." He brushed his hand through his white hair.

"Maybe not," she replied, "but look at some of these other comments he makes. 'She lived unknown and few could know/ when Lucy ceased to be/ But she is in her grave and oh/ the difference to me.' Doesn't that mean that he thinks the crime will go undetected?

And look at this one. In 'She was a phantom of delight,' there's a morbid description of her death: "I see with eye serene/ the very pulse of the machine;/ A being breathing thoughtful breath/ A traveler between life and death.'....And I think it was premeditated. It's predicted in these lines: 'Hers shall be the breathing balm/ And hers the silence and the calm/ Of mute insensate things...'"

"But surely, Miss Dixon," Shelburn was bewildered, "what... possible...reason..."

"I was getting to that," she chimed. She leaned forward and whispered: "I think it was domestic abuse. He seems real domineering. Listen to these: 'Myself will to my darling be/ Both law and impulse...the girl/ Shall feel an overseeing power...and beauty born of murmuring sound/ shall pass into her face.' It sounds like a real oppressive relationship. Check this: 'A perfect woman nobly planned/ to warn, to comfort and command'.' She looked over the top of her glasses mimicing him. "He sounds like a real sicko, Dr. Shelburn, and you know a lot of psychopaths write poetry."

"But I'm sure you're not going to find anything conclusive on this... this," he fumbled for the right words, "I mean, after all you've taken these quotes out of context. Isn't it nature doing the talking in those domineering parts, Wordsworth's personification of nature? And that makes perfect sense within the poem." He fingered the pipe on his desk nervously.

"But that's the point." Tracy's voice hushed with intense seriousness, "That's what psychopaths do. They divert responsibility for their actions. They blame it on external things, on forces greater than themselves. They hear voices of stones and mountains and things telling them what to do."

"But Wordsworth?" Shelburn pleaded, "Surely not Wordsworth."

Tracy stared straight into his eyes with an intense strength of conviction and said with confidence: "Someone killed Lucy and I intend to find out whom."

"Who," corrected Shelburn.

"Right, Who," added Tracy.

"But surely you don't think that...

"Oh, but I do, Dr. Shelburn, I do." She spoke calmly but firmly still gazing into his bewildered face.

Unable to convince Tracy of the folly of her undertaking, and in the interest of ultimately salvaging Wordsworth's reputation through what he was sure would be a futile and unproductive research, Shelburn agreed reluctantly to sanction her investigation. Any evidence would surely be only of the present circumstantial order. What could she possibly discover? After all, critics had been trying to identify Lucy for generations without success. He sat dazed and absent mindedly lit his pipe, forgetting the ban on smoking in offices. The Romantic sublime seemed suddenly like a quagmire of quicklime sucking him downward into the darker abyss of gothic horror. He seemed to envision it all now layed out before him. There was the matter of those extended gaps in the poet's sister's journals and according to later biographies; times when Wordsworth just disappeared, no one knew where.

Then too, there was Coleridge's ridiculous theory that Lucy was Wordsworth's sister, Mary—an alibi offered by a close friend no doubt. DeQuincy had the outlandish idea that Wordsworth had a secret lover, a crime of passion perhaps. And then there was "the spontaneous overflow of powerful emotion" by Wordsworth's own admission the very inspiration for poetry. Of course, the morbid fascination for epitaphs weighed heavily against the popular image of a pastoral nature poet. What could be said in defense of one who began one of the Lucy poems with "Strange fits and passions I have known" and ended it with "O Mercy! to myself , If Lucy should be dead?" That last line does seem rather strange, he reflected. If "mercy" were taken literally, why would it be merciful to the narrator if Lucy should die? But it couldn't be: it was all just too outlandish.

Shelburn put out the pipe and pulled a volume from the shelf by the window, opening it to the Wordsworth section. The words of "The Forsaken," a poem written contemporaneously with the Lucy poems had raced through his mind. There it was on the page.

The peace which others seek they find;
The heaviest storms not longest last;
Heaven grants even to the guiltiest mind
An amnesty for what is past;
When will my sentence be reversed?...
I only pray to know the worst;
And wish as if my heart would burst.

One naturally envisions an abandoned wife awaiting a wayward husband, but it's very vague. A lover's death is a forsaking too. What does the narrator feel guilty about? It might indeed be interesting, he pondered, to see just what Tracy would come up with.

The remaining weeks passed quickly, as page after page of poetry had lapped its way on to the shore and dissipated in the sand. Shelburn knew he would not drown in the abysmal sea of discontent after all. There was a log to cling to; not the one he had usually looked for, but a saving grace nonetheless. There was something refreshing in nonmajors after all—the childlike innocence—witnessing the first awakening of poetic sensibilities like the first crocus of May, or was it the first circus in July? He wasn't always sure which.

The final papers, too, had folded themselves one after another into the past complete with Dr Shelburn's evaluation, with only one remaining; the one he had put off intentionally until the end; the one he most looked foreward to; the one he most dreaded reading.

Tracy's paper began with a quote from Jerome McGann: "Romantic poems tend to develop different sorts of artistic means with which to occlude and disguise their own involvement in a certain nexus of historical relations," and from there, developed a dosier of Lucy. It was admittedly a difficult task, as Shelburn anticipated. The only evidence being primarily what Wordsworth himself wrote in the poetry. But a dosier was created. Some critics thought she may have been the Lucy Grey of earlier poems, but this was unlikely. She was young and described variously as "child" or "maiden" and her "virgin bosom" was just beginning to "swell." She had "dusky" hair. Wordsworth's attraction to her is obvious from the Romantic descriptions which seem to lack precise detail. "Eyes as stars of twilight fair," reveals more about how Lucy seemed to the poet than how she appeared to the rest of the world. She most certainly must have lived, judging from the "hilltop cottage," "apple orchard," and "Springs of Dove" references, somewhere near Dove Crag in the hills surrounding the Dovedale, Westmorland regions near Penrith, in the Lake District, where Wordsworth had visited in 1788 when he was eighteen years old, and where he lived for three years 1792-5.

Perhaps her "death" was merely poetic. Perhaps she married someone else and was merely lost to the young Wordsworth. In any case, four years later she is described as "in her grave." Wordsworth, of course went on to become the great poet and pillar of the Anglican religion, believing that "man's wild spirits needed taming by the church." One can only speculate about the origins of this conversion: whether it was his own "wild spirit" which ultimately "sealed" Lucy's slumber. Perhaps it is all merely figurative. Perhaps all men have a Lucy somewhere in their past.

But the best was yet to come. If her research was thorough, and her comments interesting and insightful, her conclusion was disconcerting. Who killed Lucy? It was, Tracy claimed, none other than Lester Shelburn himself, along with Herbert Hartman, along with a conspiracy of other notable literary dons who had chauvinistically chosen to focus attention on Wordsworth's poetics and philosophy as disembodied abstractions and ignored the hard reality of a rustic peasant girl whose death may well have inadvertently inspired an entire Romantic movement. "It seems always thus," she concluded, "the woman behind the man is negated so the man can claim the inspiration as his own."

Shelburn rested his head on his hands. The stiching on his coat cuff had become threadbare and unraveled over the semester. It was indeed, a harsh indictment, even more so because it was unexpected. It was not the quality of aesthetic appreciation he had hoped to instill in his students; far from it indeed. It was not what one would call an orthodox English paper. Yet he had to admit, it was meticulous, thorough, and interesting. It did indeed reflect a certain poetic quality and a sincere voice. No one else in the world could have written it. The argument was well formulated; if anything, erring on the side of overdetermination. "Ah, at last, imagination," he sighed sadly at the irony, "for once then, something." "A fine job," he was forced to reluctantly write on the final page. Nor was he entirely unaware of a vague sense of poetic justice in the act.

He sat defeated, weary and somber as if the flagship of the fleet had been sunk, and the war itself had been lost. As he turned the final page over, he noticed Tracy in a blue campus security uniform, standing shyly just outside the open door.

"I got on work study," she giggled.

"Well, don't just stand there. Come in. Sit down. And congratulations by the way on a fine research paper."

"Thank you," Tracy said hesitantly, "I wasn't sure you'd like it...I had second thoughts...Maybe I overstated my case a bit."

"Then you're in good company," he laughed; then in a quiet voice said, "You know, I've been doing it for years."

They both laughed at acknowledgement of a private joke, and after a brief silence Tracy announced, "I've just signed up for your class next fall."

"Oh, really?" Shelburn tried to conceal the surprise. "Which one? The Nineteenth Century Poetry?" He could see the enthusiasm build in her eyes.

"Yeah," she said. "I'm on a hot case."

"A...a hot case" he repeated suspiciously. " And what might that be—What indeed?" he demanded."

"Browning's Last Dutchess," she tossed out.

"And...WHAT...specifically concerning...Browning's Last Dutchess?" He spaced his words with deliberation and leaned forward, gripping the arms of his chair with elbows out and glared threateningly over the top of his glasses.

"Well...ah...you know," she fidgeted nervously. "Who killed her. What's the motive?"

Shelburn sat back dumbfounded once again, grasping for words in a sea of unfathomable depths."Am I to presume," he hesitated, not sure if he really wanted to know. "Am I to presume, then that you don't think it was the Duke? After all, he as much as confesses doesn't he? So...it's an open and shut case, isn't it?"

Tracy smiled. Shelburn had taken the bait. With renewed seriousness she leaned forward to whisper, for his ears only, "I think it was all a set up."

"B-But," he tried to object, but the words died on his lips as she resumed. "The way I see it it can't be the Duke...too obvious...He wants us to believe he did it a little too much to be convincing. It's never the obvious suspect you know."

Shelburn rocked his recliner back and thought for a moment, realizing he could not win. "I confess I've never quite thought of it in that light before...hmm...So you suppose," he continued, "that he's covering for someone?"

"It's possible," she admitted. But, I'm way ahead of that. For awhile I thought so to."

"Ahh," Shelburn's interest was rising. "But you no longer think so?" he baited.

"Oh, no." She stated merrily, and then waited. She knew she had his interest and would play the line before landing it.

"Well?" he prodded impatiently.

She leaned forward again staring into his face to better gage his response. "I think it was all faked," she said.

"What was faked?

"The painting," she replied. "I don't think the Duke was ever really married at all. He just didn't want to marry the new girl—got cold feet. So, he plants this fake picture see, and claims it's his old wife and he did her in. So that would make the new girl's old man object to the wedding.

"Ah, yes...I begin to see," Shelburn pondered, putting his elbow on the desk and stroking his chin. He thought a moment. "Unless..." he ventured, "Unless he really did kill her and made the blatant confession in the hope that it wouldn't be believed and would thus steer people into thinking he was covering for someone else."

"Oh my God," she gasped, "I never thought of that. I'll have to check it out!"

Shelburn coughed into his hand to stifle his embarsssment, hardly believing that he had been charmed or duped into encouraging such an outlandish pursuit—again.

"Well, I'll see you in the fall then," Tracy said rising to her feet.

Shelburn glanced out the window. The sun was fading. It was late afternoon of the last day of the semester. "I think you'll make a fine detective someday," he whispered watching the sun go down.

"Oh, I've decided to shoot for prosecuting attorney," she tossed over her shoulder as she stood up.

"Heaven help the bad guys," he thought with a smile. "Indeed, heaven help us all."

When she had gone, he stood up from the comfortable chair and pocketed his pipe. He took one last look around the office to make sure he hadn't forgotten anything. There on the shelf was a biography of Browning and a collected poetry volume. "I'd best study these over the summer," he thought, "and meticulously too." Then the haunting voice came again: "That time of life thou mayest in me behold when yellow leaves or few or none do hang..."

"But not today," he said aloud. "Too much work to do. And I should probably look into whether Marlowe wrote Shakespeare before winter too." He slid the books into his case and proceeded down the hall, out into evening glow and across the commons to his home. "Mental note to self,' he thought: "Buy a new jacket." With the wind at his back, the late sun warm on his collar, it was clear sailing until fall.

William Shakespeare

CHAPTER 8

Kathy Skomski

Where I'm From

I travel backwards north and west
to Saskatchewan prairies and mountains beyond
where my soul is painted in pine, my spirit infused with evergreen.
Mountain wisdom rumbling down like an avalanche
buries me in the sudden awareness of my small existence
amid this splendor and magnificence.
My universe realigns.
I celebrate on a pinhead in the Valley of the Ten Peaks.

Bear Mania

"You Are In Bear Country?" read the brochure handed to us by the cheerful park ranger. "We're in WHAT country?" I panicked, the thought never having crossed my mind that we might actually see a bear. This camping trip to the Tunnel Mountain Campground in Banff National Park in the Canadian Rockies was suddenly taking on a new and very disturbing dimension. "I'm not prepared for a bear," I thought. I mean, what do you do if you come in contact with one? I became instantly consumed with thoughts of bears on patrol in the park, waiting to attack unsuspecting visitors from Royal Oak, Michigan. The ranger had matter-of-factly mentioned in a we-deal-with-this-every-day kind of voice that a bear had been spotted multiple times over the past few days by campers in OUR campground and that the park rangers would be attempting to trap it that very night. This information was a double-edged sword for me. Yes, I took comfort in knowing that efforts were being launched to capture this killer, yet the bulls-eye on our tent caused me to break into a sweat.

As we located our campsite, I continued obsessing over bears. "How do you trap a bear?" I nervously quizzed my husband, Terry. "I mean, do they put out bait?" Would a bear actually come near quiet campers, like we intend to be tonight?"

"Slow down. These rangers know what they're doing. Don't worry," he said, trying to soothe my nerves. I pondered his words as we set up our tent, still very anxious about the way things might unravel during the night. We prepared our dinner, although I didn't have much of an appetite. It annoyed me watching Terry relaxing and enjoying his meal, especially when he dug into the Oreos, recklessly dropping crumbs onto the ground, seemingly oblivious to the vicious predator in the area.

As dusk began moving in, the park ranger rode up on his horse. "Hey folks, just want to remind you that we're going to try our hardest to get that bear tonight. That sucker's been giving us a real run for the money," he chortled. "You'll want to store all food in your car—don't leave anything in your tent—and be sure to clean up after yourselves before retiring for the night. Have a good rest," he said as he winked, nodded, and ambled off to the next campsite.

"Oh God, Oh God, Oh God" I thought as another wave of panic surged through my body. At that very moment, if I could have scrubbed the dirt where those damn Oreo crumbs had fallen, I would have. Instead, I cursed Terry for his carelessness and, with the sole of my shoe, worked those crumbs into the ground. I knew there would be no sleep for me that night. After all, someone had to remain on guard.

Too nervous to really take in the surrounding beauty, I was at least able to notice the orange sun sinking fast, the smell of campfires blending with the alpine air.

"Let's go for a walk. You know, check out the rest of the campground," Terry cheerfully proposed.

The idea of a little excursion briefly eased my fears as we headed out. Knowing I loved flowers, Terry made a point of calling my attention to the wild pink orchids and yellow cinquefoil that appeared in abundance along the path as we made our way toward the Bow River. I, in the meantime, was taking a mental inventory of possible bear hiding spots and the many devil-may-care campers who seemed completely unfazed by the ravenous grizzly lurking in our campground. My commitment to guard duty became even more pressing.

Darkness was now fully upon us, the dying campfires our only light as we headed back to our site. It was time to hunker down for the night. There was Terry, yawning and stretching. "Wow. I'm bushed. C'mon. Let's go to bed," he said. Reluctantly, I crawled into our impending chamber of death. Within moments of climbing into our sleeping bags, Terry was snoring like a drunk. I, on the other hand, felt as though I had just consumed three espressos, alert and antsy. Because the neglectful park ranger failed to disclose to me in detail the exact step-by-step process they would undertake in capturing this killer bear, I was left to my own devices to formulate a strategy for its entrapment. Eventually, though, pure exhaustion crept in as I began drifting into a restless slumber. Visions of an 800-pound bear lumbering toward our flimsy Coleman tent raced through my brain.

Delirium was getting the best of me as I clearly saw the morning's newspaper headlines: "LARGEST GRIZZLY BEAR IN PARK HISTORY VICIOUSLY MAULS ROYAL OAK WOMAN." It was at that very moment Terry sat up, stretched, and sleepily announced, "Move. I gotta get out and go pee."

"No. No. Please don't leave me," I pleaded. "The bear might be out there."

"Move over," he repeated, deaf to my words.

The potty break unfolded without incident as Terry quickly returned to our tent, falling back to sleep almost instantly. I, however, remained vigilant in my self-imposed guard duty. Again, I began drifting only to be brought back to my senses by a low grumbling outside the tent. I slowed my breathing, paralyzed by fear.

"Terry," I tried to whisper, "stop snoring. I think the bear is outside our tent," I managed to quietly choke out. Not wanting to move, I lay stiff and silent until dawn began breaking.

Thankfully, morning arrived without incident and in a fleeting moment of confidence, I quietly unzipped the tent flaps, took a cursory look around our campsite, and made my exit into the morning's light. It was then that I spotted animal droppings within inches of our tent.

"Oh, God. It was here," I concluded as a new wave of panic quickly set in. Terry, then, too, came crawling out of the tent with a refreshed look on his face.

"I slept like a baby. Really, it must be that mountain air," he happily exclaimed.

"Look right there by your feet. Droppings!!" I uttered.

"Oh, yeah. Looks like we had a visitor last night. Probably an elk," Terry answered, making his way to the car to retrieve the cooler. "Want breakfast?"

The rest of our camping vacation pretty much went this way only now, after such a terrifying first night, I decided that any attempts at sleep would, from this point on, take place in the backseat of our '81 Plymouth hatchback. I squeezed in some car naps during the day as we drove through the park on our way to hiking and sight-seeing, all in an attempt to be sharp for the night ahead. And even though the Tunnel Mountain grizzly had been captured that first night, I wasn't about to tempt fate by adopting a nonchalant attitude. I would just have to adjust my vacation plans and sleep patterns accordingly.

Mother Mountain

I stand here, striking the same pose I've held for thousands of years, knowing you will flock around, near, and on me with your cameras, tents, hiking boots, backpacks, and walking sticks. My crown is snow-covered, my gown adorned in pine and poplar. Although my rock face shows deep cracks and chips, evidence of landslides, irregular formations and rough surfaces, I remain solid under all conditions.

I invite you to scale my heights, breath in my musky, earthy smells, listen to the deafening sounds of my thundering cascades rushing over rocks, under fallen trees, through gullies, down cliffs, into deep whirling pools of foamy snow-melt. Photograph my rapids and blue ice cutting their way under rocky overhangs and craggy outcrops. Film my tree roots and sideways branches that provide launch pads and bridges.

As you make your way up and along my dirt-rock paths, take notice of the Indian Paintbrush, the fireweed, the wild roses, their roots securely nestled among the beds of dried pine needles and decomposing leaves. Pause to look skyward through the pine boughs at the pieces of crystal blue sky and sun rays trying hard to penetrate the dense canopy, desperate to reach my floor. Watch for chipmunks darting and posing, darting and posing, and if you're quick enough you might even manage a close-up of one perched on a boulder.

I am home to many animals whose hiding places remain my secret. At times, you will spot a mountain goat, a long-horn sheep, an elk, or even a black bear foraging for food in my kitchen. They do best fending for themselves as I provide all they could ever want and need to sustain them. Most are camera shy, but many will linger along my base nourishing themselves on scrub brush and grass.

When you grow weary, needing to catch your breath and rest your sore feet, find comfort on my strong hips. Lean on me, close your eyes, and let me lull you to sleep. I'll be here tomorrow. *Shhhhhh. Shhhhhh.*

CHAPTER 9

Patricia Guest

The Perfect Gift

My husband did not marry me for my ability to select the perfect gift. On his nineteenth birthday, my very first present to him was an ugly plaid flannel shirt. I spent hours at the Gap, wishing his birthday was not between summer season and fall fashions, and selected the best of the offerings. He sweetly pretended to like it, although I am not sure that he ever actually wore it. Unfortunately, the plaid flannel shirt set the tone for the next twelve birthdays and Christmases. I somehow always found the most practical, banal offerings at the mall. Macy's gift giving guide was not much of a help, nor were his mother's suggestions. Admitting defeat, we decided this past Christmas to pool our money and buy something practical for the house.

A few days after Christmas, though, I had found the ideal gift, one he was waiting for, but did not expect. Far from practical or useful, opening this gift would bring the same happiness he felt as an eight-year-old tearing the paper off his GI Joe Aircraft Carrier. I wrapped it in recycled tissue paper and placed it in a snowman bag.

Controlling my impulse to call him at work and ruin the surprise was easy that day. A winter storm had knocked out power lines, so we had neither heat nor electricity. My resistance to subscribe to cellular phone service was finally paying off. Thanks to a generous class, we had a gift card to the Downtown Andiamo's restaurant and had already decided to take advantage of the free meal and warm venue.

As his arrival home drew near, I zipped up my fancy boots and snapped the last button on my skirt closed. I practiced looking happy for our outing, but not so excited that he would be suspicious. Breathing deeply to calm my nerves, my hands gently skimmed my abdomen; a smile immediately sprung up on my face. I peeked behind the curtains, waiting for his car. When he finally pulled up, I clutched the small bag in my hand and pulled the door closed with the other.

Subduing my giddiness became more of a challenge as we drove down Lakeshore through Grosse Pointe towards Detroit. My teeth clenched the edge of my lower lip as my eyes alternated between the bag on the floor and the twinkling Christmas lights. Steve talked about his research, and I asked the usual follow up questions, just as I would do any other night.

Finally he parked the car on the deserted downtown street. As he fumbled for a quarter to feed the meter, I reached for the bag. Before he could exit, I said "Oh, I have a late Christmas gift for you."

"Oh, great," he replied, his voice dripping with sarcasm, "is it going to be something I'll actually like?" The paper crunched as he moved it around, searching for the mysterious gift. His head suddenly darted in my direction, then back to the bag. My smile grew larger as his jaw fell open.

"So, two pink lines means…"

"Yep."

"But I thought…"

"Well, we thought wrong. We got lucky."

He stroked his left hand though his hair, still looking at the small plastic stick in his right. Disbelief and happiness spun across his face.

"So, do you actually like it?"

I think he'll keep this present around longer than the plaid flannel shirt.

School Supplies

It was a hot, humid Thursday. Not much planned for the afternoon, just a quick trip to Target for cleaning supplies and shaving cream. An artificially cool breeze welcomed me at the entrance. I grabbed a red cart and wheeled my way past women's clothing, lingerie, and kids' shoes. I rounded the corner, disappointed in the lack of new maternity shirts, but then saw it in the distance.

Twenty five yards in the distance, ten feet off the ground stood the sign. Each poster-sized letter was written on yellow notebook paper: *Back to School Supplies*. I gasped. I was expecting this moment, just not so soon. I weaved my cart in between the lady debating between black and argyle socks and the man selecting new boxer briefs. The scrub brushes my husband needed sat untouched on the shelf. The signed pulled me to the back corner of the store, blinding me to the desires of all others. Dishes be damned! New colored pencils were just feet away.

My heart all aflutter, I picked up the Crayola crayons. Twenty-five cents for a pack of fresh crayons. I knew what lay inside: twenty-four perfectly sharpened colors from marigold to indigo. I could see my future students in stiff new shirts pressing their precious September crayons ever so gently on crisp white paper to draw a perfect border. Unlike the lackluster June crayons with their smushed tops, held by sweaty kids in stained t-shirts, these beauties offer all the colors in a perfectly pointed array. And now all for just twenty-five cents. I stashed two-dozen boxes in my cart as I eyed the markers.

The markers. Eight count. Traditional colors. In my mind I saw my students drawing lines with the ideal thickness without even a hint of fading. The titles to stories, their names on the back to school poster, everything would be written in sharp, bold color, just as Crayola promises. Throughout the year the markers would be cast aside, unloved after overuse, but now, the eight cylinders full of vivid magic, sat on sale at Target. Soon, ten lucky packages would be waiting patiently in the supply cabinet of Room 102.

Notebooks without ripped pages and two-pocket portfolios that have yet to be crushed in a backpack between peanut butter sandwiches and half-eaten apples lay at the end of the aisle. I tapped my finger on my cart behind a child debating between purple and red, frantic that she would for some reason snag all twenty five cases of notebooks that I need to color coordinate my students' reading journals. Finally it was my turn. Pushing the markers and crayons aside, I made room for my latest desire, and moved on.

Six packs of erasers for two dollars and fifty seven cents each (that is less than thirty cents each!), glue sticks with their caps on, and school boxes with their snapped lids still snapped rounded out my shopping binge. Totally content, my heavy cart and I made it to the check out.

I sighed as I stuck my key in the ignition on my way home. My pulse slowed down. Over a hundred dollars worth of school supplies sat in my backseat, eager to help create a coordinated classroom for 20 eight-year-olds. The rest of summer will be cherished by all, but the promise of high-quality, discounted school supplies waiting on the desks brightens the idea of going back to school.

CHAPTER 10
Renée Reznik

Where I Am From

I am from the verdant hills
From generations way back
I am from 100 acres of land
Where my ancestors dwelled

I am from Morning Glories
Gently saluting the sunrise in all their splendor
Cherry trees and raspberry bushes inviting me to taste
From freshly baked tomato pies
Habichuelas
Arroz con gandules
And the tantalizing aroma of beef roast
Dressed in fresh herbs
So tender
So succulent

I am from summer vacations
From Sea World
Reluctantly holding my first starfish
From MGM Studios
Wide-eyed and daydreaming of becoming an actress
From Californian beaches
Collecting seashells along the shoreline
From Disney World
Desperately seeking Mickey, Minnie, Donald and the rest of the crew

I am from Costa Rican hikes at dawn as the sun awoke from its
slumber
From across the plains to the Caribbean waters and the sand beneath
my feet
Nostalgia
Hoopla
Exhilaration
Loud incessant giggling
Family memories embedded in my psyche

I am from afternoon naps with bisabuela, my great-grandmother
Inhaling her virtue
Never taking her for granted
From a stuffy attic with a cedar chest full of keepsakes
A gold locket given to Abuelita at 15 and passed on to me when I turned the same
A silent quinceañera between grandmother and granddaughter

I am from the twirl of Wonder Woman
And the snap of her golden whip for justice
I am from the martial arts Bruce Lee infused in me
From Judy Blum novels asking the question *Are You There God it's me, Margaret?*
Replacing her name and inserting my own
From the movie *Fame* starring Irene Cara
Embodied her as my alter ego
Boricua, dancing and completely free

I am from running through school halls shouting with Tears for Fears
Living off the Wall with Michael Jackson
Driving my little red corvette with Prince
Oh, wait a minute
Actually my corvette was blue

I am from John McEnroe's tennis fever
Winning the citywide championship three years in a row
Rocking out with Duran Duran's John Taylor
Long hair
Strong jaw line
Such alluring looks
From a serious infatuation with John Stamos
Obsessively plastered posters all over my walls
I am from John 1:1
Connected to God
Embracing His eternal word
Never forgetting how to be lively and laughable
After all He has a sense of humor too
I guess I had a thing for guys named John

I am from Michigan
In the middle of the cold winter
While my spirit was born in Puerto Rico
Where the palm trees sway in the breeze
Celebrating my actuality
I am from one end of the spectrum to the other
Very different
Unique
Yet all intertwined with me

I am from the strong
Of great endurance
I am from no point of return
Moving forward and accomplishing my goals

Horizon

An invisible line appears to intersect the
contrasting blues of the water from the sky.
Yet their seamlessness gives the illusion that they are one.

The sparkling sapphire on top of turquoise flowing forward
touching my feet as each wave washes on shore.
Standing here with sand between my toes.

The gentle fingers of a breeze sweep through my hair.
Many times have I seen your image unfold
from the neat crease dividing the sea from above
like the simple beauty of pictures without frames.

You are my Horizon above the many currents
connecting me to the heavens.
I've tried to escape you but find myself
back on the shoreline surrendering.

Instead of witnessing the sun slip away for another
night's slumber. I watch you, The Son, glide over
waves to shine tender rays on my face.

Strangely, I want to flee as you step
from the last stream of ripples.
Somehow the sand anchors my feet firm.
Your caress draws me close.
There are no boundaries between us.

That subtle line drawn across the sky
dramatically reveals our indivisibility.
Such connectedness pushes back the shades
of indigo to step ashore purifying my feet as
waves continuously accumulate beneath me.
My Horizon—a line forever encircling my heart.

Misinterpretations

She had maternal passion
that was somehow mistaken
as being ogre like.
Funny though considering her
charm turned heads constantly.

Motherly attributes may have
pushed aside his affection.
Could have been a constant
reminder of his own mother
whom he had not favored.

Always secretly desiring a
parachute but fearing the
turbulence; thus, he never did
soar beyond his wing span.
Sadly keeping his gate sealed shut
to great possibilities even love.

But she, the misconstrued one,
was hurt before by unforeseen betrayal.
Perhaps the unanticipated escapade
was responsible for misinterpretations.

It was a man she had loved deeply and
in the quiet of the night her heart trills
incessantly seeking solace from all the pain.
Wishing that her desire to give from a deep
And pure place would be embraced not shunned.

Zebra

I remember being called Casper, Cracker, and Zebra.
I am neither white nor black and white.
No accurate boxes selected.
No global sensibility.
No multicultural awareness.
No regard for my true identity.
No amiable clichés for quick summary.
Crayon, chalk, pencil shavings
And the scent of stuffy classrooms all filled my nostrils.
My stomach sank, twisted and turned
As if on a rollercoaster.
Strawberry Lollipops on my tongue suppressed my sustained silence.
Moist meticulous hands nervously tugged at my pleated skirt.
Pleat by pleat, one by one, crumple by crumple.
Increased heart palpitations stuck in my throat.
Stationary feet, immovable, firmly planted.
Twirling transient thoughts desperately seeking refuge.
Without giddiness or bliss, the playground spun like a carousel.
Individual faces blurred as one.
Shades of brown all around
Pointing fingers and laughing along.
I'd escape their torment humming my favorite song.

Sheila

Laughter. Two girls jumping rope. One. Two. Three. Three brothers playing a chasing game. The youngest is giggling as his short legs don't allow him to catch up to his older brothers.

Sheila wags her tail as the temptation calls her across the street. So many neighbors enjoying this wonderful day. Waves. Greetings. Peace is thick in the air.

The sun feels hot as its rays blanket the neighborhood. Mrs. Whitman always took advantage of these sun filled days with her multitude of flowers in front of her house. Such as usual mix. Tulips. Sunflower. Ferns. Flower in small pots. Big pots. Dangling flowers from hanging vines. Flower beds all lined up like soldiers in front of the windows.

Even though we had tons of flowers surrounding our house the scent of hers tickled my nose as I stood on our porch peering down the street. That's when I saw the black car. Moving like a stallion coming around the corner.

Once the turn was complete the car fishtailed. Fast. Way too fast. Too early in the day with so many kids out. Slow down, Mister. But no! His foot got heavier on the pedal as it screeched down the street. Burning rubber pushed aside the sweet aroma of Mrs. Whitman's floral arrangement.

Everyone seemed to notice. Except Sheila. She sees me standing on the porch. I can't descend. Don't move, I think. Everyone is frozen. Frozen like ice. No one melts from this frozen state even though it's a hot day. Everyone. Everything suspended in time. Except for Sheila and the zooming car. Tires spinning. Dust flying.

She doesn't notice the fright on all of our faces. She smiles at me and wants to return home. No Sheila. No. Stay frozen. Don't move. Stay with the boys!

As she moved toward the curb, the boys tried grabbing her and telling her to stay put. I yell, "No Sheila! Stay there!" She doesn't listen. Perhaps she didn't hear.

Like a black stallion on an open field the car continued with the steady momentum. Voices. Shrills. Shout outs for Sheila not to run all intertwined with the growl of the engine quickly approaching.

Stubborn Sheila bolted forward. Her determination relentless. Boundless. Undeterred as she sprang into the street. The force of speed pushing forward had all of hair blow backwards and bounce up and down with each stride.

Fast. Way too fast. Too early in the day with too many kids out. Slow down mister. Sheila is crossing the street.

The black stallion's face pressed forward anyhow. It never slowed. It didn't care. Simply moved like it was on an open field.

Stampede. Collision. Crash. She's been hit. Pressure surrounded my heart. My knees weakened as I gripped the banister tightly. Screams. Continuous screams. My six-year-old voice is heard three blocks away.

Not my Sheila. Please no. Shrills. Cries of pain from Sheila as she dashed for the porch tore at my throat. Tugged on my heart. She's limping. Blood. Drops of blood trail behind her. Blood stains the porch steps leading to the door.

The black stallion never slowed. Never looked back. Never apologized. Never blinked an eye. It continued to move like it was on an open field.

CHAPTER 11

Lisa Hine

A Tribute

You endured 48 hours of hard labor,
Panting, suffering,
Alone.
For that, I thank you.

You tried to control my decisions,
My boyfriends, my mistakes,
Me.
For that, I forgive you.

You shared with me your life, your mistakes,
Your triumphs.
Everything.
For that, I know you.

You stayed in an unhappy marriage,
Oppressive, bleak.
You settled.
For that, I pity you.

You portrayed confidence, demanded equality,
Asserted yourself.
Boldly.
For that, I envy you.

You persisted in reaching your goals,
Never quit.
Relentless.
For that, I admire you.

You gave me your time, your love,
Your guidance.
Selflessly.
For that, I love you.

He Said, She Said

She said:
"He pushed me! He did!
He ran up from behind me and clunked me on the head!"

He said:
"She started it! She did!
She stole my new video game and won't give it back!"

She said:
"He's mean! He is!
He's got skinny legs, wired glasses—
A Harry Potter imposter!"

He said:
"She's a brat! She is!
She's got pigtails, she's toothless, but she's a devil inside!"

I say:
"They're clever! They are!
Master manipulators disguised in four foot packages."

And then…

"They're children. They are.
Calm down, breathe deeply,
September can't be THAT far."

CHAPTER 12

Shaun Moore

Seven-Words Poem

Smoke from the teepees,
signaled the blame.
They fought for their freedom;
All we did was maim.

The village was hazy,
death shrills filled the air.
A jasper bracelet here,
A child's ragged doll, there.

Bodies purple and putrid,
the stench was so great.
No human beings
should be dealt this fate.

Yet we stacked them up high,
thick blood cascading free.
And when the fires burned out,
their people ceased to be.

Alphabet Poem 1

Another battle,
craving death.
Everyone finds great hope
in justified killing.
Lying monarchs,
nervous, oppressed people
Quixotic rebels sate themselves
under violent war,
executing young zealots.

Alphabet Poem 2

All boys can detect
envious females.
Great heroes,
invoking jesters
keeping lusts mummed
now oscillating purposefully
Quick repetition.
Silent treatment.
Underwear viewing.
We experience youthful zen.

Fountain Square

The afternoon sun shown
The dried up fountain anticipated
The flag at half mast mourned
The shadows from the trees masked
The construction banged and clanged

Yet I did not

Students could wander and talk
Wind could blow the breeze
Flowers could spring to life
Lamps could look down
Trees could grow their roots

Yet I could not

I could not sing like the birds
I could not bring light into the world
I could not change the weather
I could not utter a word

For I was the fountain square

I could support the curious bodies
I could bubble up like waves to become seats
I could offer rest to weary travelers

I'd like to see the sun do that

I'm in Charge of Crafting Worlds

Sometimes people ask me, aren't you lonely down there, writing in the basement? Sure, it's a small hole in the ground that I call my office, where the light barely trickles in through the one small window just above my computer. And while there may not be another living soul in the house, I don't get lonely when I'm writing. How could I? I'm in charge of crafting worlds.

I never understood people who didn't like writing, who weren't fascinated with it. I'm sure everyone is prone to daydreaming every now and again, letting their mind wander away from them and playing on the fancies that run through their heads. I know it's a favorite pastime of mine, and one which often leads me to great story ideas. But the true fun comes in the form of writing them out, letting them expand on the screen as I type blindly away, never sure where this story is taking me, but always full of wonder at where I find myself in the end.

I believe I get a little drunk on power as I'm writing, for I am crafting worlds, deciding fates, imposing my will on the endless stream of characters that pour forth from my mind. I can decide on a whim whether or not someone falls in love, they get that big promotion, or they survive that horrible crash. As I am crafting, lives hang in the balance, universes bang into being, and time has no meaning.

My characters become real, growing unique personalities all their own, oftentimes running away from the idea I had in my head, or growing beyond it, like a hermit crab too big for the shell I had given it. These fictional people can grow to be as real as the memories I have of old friends, and sometimes seem even more tangible than that. They keep me guessing as to where they will be taking me, for while I am their God, I am not an omniscient being. I can even see at times that I am not always in control, and take a back seat as I let them tell the story that they want told.

So how could I be lonely, sitting in my basement, clicking away on those magical keys that spring worlds to life quicker than my fingers can tap it all out? I almost have to laugh at the thought.